SCOOBY-DOO

AND THE LOCH NESS MONSTER

Adapted by Suzanne Weyn from
the script by Douglas Wood

P9-CAN-403

WB
WORLDWIDE PUBLISHING

SCHOLASTIC INC.

New York   Toronto   London   Auckland   Sydney
Mexico City   New Delhi   Hong Kong   Buenos Aires

No part of this publication may be reproduced in whole or in part, or stored in a retrieval system, or transmitted in any form or by any means, electronic, mechanical, photo-copying, recording, or otherwise, without written permission of the publisher. For information regarding permission, write to Scholastic Inc., Attention: Permissions Department, 557 Broadway, New York, NY 10012.

ISBN 0-439-60698-5

Copyright © 2004 by Hanna-Barbera.
SCOOBY-DOO and all related characters and elements are trademarks of and © Hanna-Barbera.
(s04)
Published by Scholastic Inc. All rights reserved.
SCHOLASTIC and associated logos are trademarks and/or registered trademarks of Scholastic Inc.

Designed by Louise Bova
Printed in the U.S.A.

First printing, June 2004
12 11 10 9 8 7 6 5 4 3 2 1   4 5 6 7 8 9/0

CHAPTER ONE

"Wow! How beautiful!" Daphne Blake said as the Mystery Machine rolled over the crest of a hill. "This Scottish countryside is so lush and green!"

Fred Jones turned from his seat behind the steering wheel and nodded in agreement. "Yeah, it's just like a giant golf course," he added.

Velma Dinkly leaned forward from the back seat. She cleaned her eyeglasses on her orange turtleneck sweater and returned them to her freckled face. "If you find a scenic spot, would you pull the van over so I can take pictures?" she requested.

"It's *all* scenic," Fred remarked, letting the warm breeze from the open window ruffle his short blond hair.

Shaggy and Scooby sat beside Velma in the back seat. They peered out the window as the Scottish countryside went by. "Like, are we there yet, Freddy?" Shaggy asked.

"I don't know," he admitted.

"Jinkies, Daphne, it must be exciting for you to visit Blake Castle," Velma said. "Can you believe you're actually visiting the ancient home of your Scottish ancestors?"

"It sure *is* exciting," Daphne agreed, pushing her hair over her shoulder. "And I can't wait to help my cousin, Shannon, host the Loch Ness Highland Games. When she wrote to invite us to the games, I said we'd definitely come. This is the first time the Highland Games have been held at Blake

Castle. She's worked hard to make the ancient castle grounds into a first-rate tournament field. I even dressed for the occasion!" Daphne smoothed her plaid, pleated skirt and tossed her green scarf over one shoulder. "I'm planning to wear this for the opening ceremonies in honor of the Blakes of Loch Ness."

Daphne's relatives had lived in Loch Ness for centuries. In Scotland, loch means lake. Blake Castle was next to the famous lake the Scottish people call Loch Ness.

"Like, it's not the *Blakes* of Loch Ness I'm worried about," Shaggy remarked. As he spoke he shivered fearfully. Scooby-Doo, Shaggy's Great Dane, moved closer to him and also gave a quick, fearful shake.

Velma nodded knowingly. "Are you

by chance referring to the legend of the Loch Ness Monster?" she asked. "The monster the locals call Nessie?"

"Ronster!" Scooby cried, terror-stricken. If there was one thing that Shaggy and Scooby did not want to hear anything about, it was monsters. They were cowards — and proud of it! They would much prefer to eat a six course dinner — with Scooby Snacks after each course — than have anything to do with any more monsters. They'd already met up with more monsters than they cared to remember.

"Like, why are we going to a place that's already got a monster named after it?" Shaggy asked.

Fred grunted scornfully. "Legend of the loch — get real! It's just another big fake, right Velma?"

"I'm not so sure about that," Velma

replied. She reached under her seat and took out a thick book with a picture on the cover. The drawing showed a huge monster, a cross between a prehistoric brachiosaurus and a medieval dragon with huge, daggerlike teeth.

"Jeepers! Do you believe in the Loch Ness Monster, Velma?" Daphne asked.

"Well, I believe it's a mystery," Velma explained, flipping through her book that told all about the creature. "This monster is different than some of the others we've met up with. There have been over two thousand sightings of the Loch Ness Monster, dating all the way back to 540 A.D. That's almost fifteen hundred years ago!"

"Zoinks!" Shaggy cried. "Like, a monster that's been scaring people for more than a thousand years — who would want to keep track of something like that?"

A large lake suddenly appeared in the distance in front of them. "That's it, gang," Fred told them, "Loch Ness, dead ahead."

"Did you have to say *dead*?" Shaggy asked, his voice growing high and squeaky with fear.

When the Mystery Machine drew nearer to it, the gang could see that the lake was shimmering from the bottom of high cliffs. They were driving along a road high above it.

As they drove, the sky grew darker and clouds of misty fog rolled along the road. "I can't see a thing," Fred complained, leaning forward over the steering wheel. "It was so clear and sunny just a little while ago. Now this fog is as thick as pea soup."

Up ahead, he saw a gigantic, dark form moving through the fog. "Whoa!" Fred exclaimed softly. He leaned even closer trying to see what it was. "What *is* that?"

Velma and Daphne also strained forward, trying to see. Velma wiped her eyeglasses and peered out of the windshield, staring into the fog. "Can we get closer?" she asked.

"I'll try," Fred said, and he steered the Mystery Machine toward the dark shape that loomed ahead of them. He drove for only a minute more before he knew something was terribly wrong!

"Freddy, the road!" Daphne shouted.

Blinded by the heavy fog, Fred had driven the Mystery Machine off a cliff! "Aaaahhhh!" the gang screamed together as their van plummeted through the air toward the lake below!

The Mystery Machine hit the side of the cliff with a thud. Its tires bounced as it slid sideways. In a second, it would be in the lake.

The doors of the Mystery Machine sprang open. The gang could see the lake shimmering below them.

"Jump!" Fred shouted.

CHAPTER TWO

The Mystery Machine stood on two wheels with its hood sunk under water. "C'mon, gang," Fred said. He knew they had to get the Mystery Machine out of the water quickly. "This lake water could shrink the van's genuine vinyl seat coverings. I hope it doesn't get wet."

Daphne put a hand on Fred's arm. "What did we see out there in the fog?" she asked.

"Whatever it was, it's gone now," he replied, looking around.

A shadow across the lake caught Daphne's attention. Looking up, she saw that on the cliff above them was a gigantic stone building with towers, high walls, and flags waving in the breeze. "Guys, look!" she shouted, pointing. "I think we're here! There's Blake Castle!"

The kids left the Mystery Machine in the water and began to climb the rocky cliff. There was no way they could pull the van out of the lake without help. Hopefully someone at the castle would be able to help.

The climb was a struggle, but they finally made it to the top. Breathlessly, the gang staggered onto the grassy field outside the stone entrance to the castle. To the side of the castle were rolling grasslands. Many large tents had been set up all around.

"Jinkies! Look at all the tents!" Velma commented.

"Like, I wonder if the circus is in town," Shaggy added. "Hey, Scoob, maybe they'll get the Loch Ness Monster to perform on the trapeze!"

"That's not a circus," Velma told Scooby and Shaggy. "It's the sports field for the Highland Games, a competition featuring traditional Scottish sporting events."

Daphne and Velma walked to the edge of the nearest field and looked down at a dock on the lake below. A very large boat was tied up at the dock. It tilted badly to one side and a big chunk of its hull had been ripped out. "Jinkies!" Velma cried. "I wonder what happened."

Fred, Shaggy, and Scooby joined Daphne and Velma. "C'mon, gang, let's check it out," Fred suggested.

They headed toward the edge of the field and climbed down again. Down by the rocky shoreline, they got a better look at the torn-up boat.

As they walked out onto the dock, a slim, attractive young woman came running down the cliff toward them. She wore jeans and a long-sleeved T-shirt. Her red hair was cut short, but except for that difference, she could have been Daphne's twin. "Daphne!" she cried, spreading her arms wide in greeting. They could hear her crisp Scottish accent in the very first word she spoke.

"Shannon!" Daphne cried. A moment later, the two cousins were wrapped in a hug. "I can't believe I'm really here!" Daphne exclaimed happily.

Daphne introduced Shannon to the gang. Shannon assured them she was thrilled that they would all be staying at Blake Castle as her guests.

"What happened to your boat, Shannon?" Fred asked.

"It looks like it had a pretty hard crash," Velma added.

Shannon looked away from them unhappily. "Oh, that," she said with a sigh. "Well, um . . ." For some reason, she didn't seem to want to tell them what happened.

The gang was distracted from their question by a heavy-set young man wearing glasses who hurried along the shore toward them. He wore baggy, messy clothes and his long hair was tied back in a sloppy ponytail. "What are you people doing?" he shouted at the gang. "This whole area has to be roped off for evidence!"

Shannon rolled her eyes in dismay and waved him away. "Not now, Del," she said.

Del came up onto the dock along-side them. "We have twenty eyewit-nesses," he said, speaking in a quick, excited rush. "They saw the large wake it left! This is big — really, really big!"

Shaggy didn't think he liked the sound of that one bit. "Why can't it ever be something *small*," he asked, "something really, really *small*?"

Del heard Shaggy and threw his arms up excitedly. "Whoa! Are you kidding? This is major!" he cried. "Last night a whole group of us were on Shannon's boat when the Loch Ness Monster rose up and attacked us. Don't you see? It's because of the games. All the activity has disturbed the creature."

"Zoinks!" Shaggy cried. Now he was

certain he didn't like the sound of this.

A tall, elderly man had come along the lake's shoreline. Now he stood on the rocks by the water and pointed a bony finger at Del. "The only disturbed creature around here is you, Del Chilton!" he accused. "Why, my own sons, Angus and Colin, were out there on that boat and they're not spooked a bit!"

"That's Lachlan Haggart," Shannon whispered. "He's a local hotel owner and businessman."

Two broad-shouldered, athletic-looking young men had come up along the shore and stood behind the man. "Angus was scared," one of them said, poking the other.

"I was not, Colin!" Angus grumbled,

annoyed at his teasing brother. He grabbed Colin and trapped him in a wrestling headlock. Colin fought back, jabbing his brother in the side with closed fists.

"That's enough, lads," their father scolded. "Save it for the games."

Del stepped toward Lachlan Haggart and his sons with his arms outstretched beseechingly. "Don't you get it? We're trespassing on the monster's sacred nesting ground! We've got to cancel the games and clear out of here!"

Mr. Haggart dismissed Del's words with a scornful wave. "Are you loony, man?" he shouted. "We can't cancel the games when every hotel in the glen is filled to capacity, including my own! If you ask me, it be the Haggart family tradition of winning these games that you be fearing most, Del. That's the true reason you want the games shut down!" He turned sharply and stormed off down the shoreline. With a quick wave good-bye to Shannon, his sons ran after him.

Del whirled around to face Shannon and the gang. "Consider yourselves warned!" he told them, pointing one finger and waving it in the air dramatically. "I told you these games were a mistake, Shannon! Now the monster's after you!"

CHAPTER THREE

Shannon led the gang through the castle's tall front door. "Wow! Castle Blake!" Daphne exclaimed. "I've waited my whole life to see this." She craned her head back to look up at the 20-foot-high ceilings with their immense wooden beams. Shards of sunlight shone through the many high, stained-glass windows. Suits of armor stood along the stone walls.

"Yeah, these are some digs," Shaggy said.

"It sounds like you've had sort of a little trouble around here lately," Fred mentioned.

"It seems we have plenty of trouble here at Blake Castle," Shannon told them. "It actually began just a few nights ago. I was by myself, down at the boat dock, when all of a sudden something very big and very fast came cruising into the cove. I only saw it for a moment, then it disappeared below the surface and I lost sight of it. The next night I thought I saw something huge moving right outside the castle."

Velma recalled reports she'd read of Loch Ness Monster sightings. "I read that many people claim to have seen the Loch Ness Monster on land," she said.

"So, the monster isn't locked in the loch," Daphne remarked.

Shannon sighed deeply. "No, but the next time we saw it, it *was* in the loch. It rose up and caused the damage to my boat that you just saw. When I woke up this morning, I tried to tell myself that it was only a dream."

Suddenly, a secret passage in one of the walls began to spin. As it slowed, a woman with chin-length, auburn hair stepped out of it and into the hall. "It was no dream! Last night's shipwreck was no accident!" she said dramatically. "'Twas the great beast of the loch!"

Shannon began to introduce the woman. "Everyone, I'd like you to meet . . ."

". . . Professor Fiona Pembroke," Velma finished Shannon's sentence. "She's Scotland's most accomplished Loch Ness expert and author of the book, *Legend of the Loch*." She reached into her bag and pulled out the book she'd been reading in the Mystery Machine. She held it up and showed them all that Fiona Pembroke was its author.

"How marvelous!" Professor Pembroke said, taking the book from

Velma. She sat down in a high-back easy chair and took out a pen, preparing to sign Velma's book. "What a pleasure to meet someone who's done her proper research," she said.

Velma nodded enthusiastically. "I read that you're still trying to prove the monster exists," she said, "even though it has destroyed your scientific credibility and devastated you financially."

Professor Pembroke coughed uneasily. "Apparently too *much* research," she added. She handed the book back to Velma, unsigned. As she returned the book, three photos fell from her hand.

Velma quickly knelt to scoop them up. "Wow, professor!" she exclaimed, looking at the pictures. "These new pictures of the Loch Ness Monster are amazing!" Up until then, she wasn't sure if she thought the monster was real or not. But here was real proof! This was a truly exciting discovery!

"I was out on the loch myself when, all of a sudden, there she was — right next to my boat!" the professor recalled.

"After the world sees these photos, everyone will believe in the monster!" Velma said excitedly.

"Oh, I wish it were that easy, dear," Professor Pembroke said to Velma. "But, as you know, my scientific reputation isn't what it used to be. I'll have to wait for just the right moment to reveal them to the public. I can't afford to be laughed off again."

Professor Pembroke said good-bye to them and left. "She's staying here at the castle doing research," Shannon told them.

Shannon led the gang up a wide, stone staircase to their rooms, where they washed up. A few hours later, they met downstairs in the main dining room for dinner. It was a large, majestic space with the longest dinner table they'd ever seen.

In the center of the table sat large silver trays with domed covers.

"I've prepared a traditional Scottish dinner for ye, so you'd all get a good taste of the Highlands," Shannon explained as she reached for the first cover. She lifted the lid of the serving tray. "We'll be starting with haggis, a true Scottish delicacy," she explained. Under the cover there were six smooth, round, grayish balls. None of the gang had ever seen anything like them.

"Wow, like, what's in it?" Shaggy

asked, cautiously poking one of the balls with his fork.

"It's a sheep stomach stuffed with diced liver and kidneys, spices, and oatmeal and boiled," Shannon told him.

The gang looked at one another nervously. None of them knew if they were brave enough to try it, but they didn't want to hurt Shannon's feelings.

Just then, something zoomed into the room and banged up against the window, cracking it. "Zoinks!" Shaggy cried. "It's the monster!"

A tall man stepped into the doorway. He wore a Scottish-style hat known as a tam and a traditional Scottish kilt. He was an older man with a prominent nose and thick, bushy sideburns. "Dear me, terribly sorry about that," he apologized. "I couldn't resist tossing the caber," he added as he retrieved the pole he'd tossed right into the room.

Shannon turned to the gang. "Everyone, it's my honor to introduce the head field judge for this year's Highland Games."

Once again, Velma had done her research. "Sir Ian Locksley," she spoke up. "You're the director of the Scottish Natural History Museum and author of the book, *Monster, My Foot!*"

"Velma, do you have a book for every occasion?" Shannon asked.

"Actually," Velma replied, "yes."

"So, let me get this straight," Shaggy said. "You're a museum director and a judge for the games?"

Sir Ian nodded.

"Now that's what I call multi-tasking!" Shaggy said.

Velma had brought Sir Ian's book down to dinner with her. She now held it up for everyone to see. "Sir Ian," she said, "according to your book, you believe the Loch Ness Monster is all a bunch of hooey!"

"Yes! Yes!" he agreed emphatically. "Hooey! Nonsense! Poppycock and fiddle-faddle! As I say — *Monster, My Foot!*" Sir Ian's expression turned sour as Professor Pembroke walked into the dining hall. "Good gravy!" he cried in dismay. "What in blazes are you doing here?"

Professor Pembroke glowered at him. "Hello, Ian!" she said tartly.

"You two know each other?" Fred asked.

"Ian and I were once colleagues," Professor Pembroke told him.

"Colleagues? Hardly!" Sir Ian scoffed, his voice thick with disdain. "She was my research assistant."

"Before you had me fired!" the professor reminded him angrily.

CHAPTER FOUR

For the rest of the meal, Professor Pembroke and Sir Ian glared at one another. No one really wanted to eat the haggis and they quickly excused themselves and went to bed.

But Shaggy lay awake looking out the tall windows as a fat full moon shone on his blanket. A rumbling sound came from Scooby, who was lying next to him in the big bed. He recognized the sound because he'd heard it many times before — from his own stomach.

Shaggy shook Scooby by the shoulders, waking him. "Scoob, with your stomach growling like that, I'll never get any sleep." Shaggy got up, changing out of his pajamas and back into his clothing. "Like, how far is it to the nearest vending machine?"

Scooby followed Shaggy out into the dark, moonlit hallway. The castle was completely quiet as they padded down the stairs to the first floor. The suits of armor shone in the moonlight and the stone floor felt cold under their bare feet as they padded down the hall. "Okay! The kitchen should be right around this corner," Shaggy said.

They turned and came to another long hallway. "Did I say *kitchen*?" Shaggy asked with a laugh. "I mean creepy *hallway*. Another creepy *hallway* is right around this corner." They went down it, took another turn — and came to yet *another* long hall.

"Rikes!" Scooby cried.

"Zoinks! Like, wrong turn!" Shaggy said. He could hear Scooby's knees knocking together in reply. The castle *was* awfully dark and scary at night. And who knew where the Loch Ness Monster might be lurking? "It's okay, Scoob," Shaggy said. "Like, just keep telling yourself there's no such thing as monsters."

"Ro ronsters! Ro ronsters!" Scooby repeated nervously.

BANG! Something crashed against the outside of the nearest window. "Ronster! Ronster!" Scooby shouted in terror as he leapt into Shaggy's arms.

"Like, boy, do I hope you're wrong!" Shaggy said. *Bangbangbang!* Something knocked at the window again — and suddenly, Shaggy realized what was making the noise. "Look, Scooby-Doo," he said with a laugh as he set Scooby down. "It's just a tree branch knocking against that window. That's nothing to be afraid of."

Scooby looked up and saw that Shaggy was right. "Ree-hee-hee," he giggled, feeling foolish.

Shaggy's stomach grumbled, reminding him of why they were standing in the hallway of this eerie, dark castle in the middle of the night. "Now, the kitchen's got to be around here somewhere," he said. "Let's try down this way."

"Rokay," Scooby agreed. Together they explored the hallway in front of them. In the dark, it looked very much like the hallway they'd just left.

RUMBLE! BANG! A boom of thunder seemed to shake the castle. Scooby yelped with fright.

"Now, stay close, buddy," Shaggy

advised. His voice was shaky, even though he was trying to sound brave. "We don't want anything scary sneaking up on —"

Lightning lit the sky — and a horrible monstrous face stared in the window at them!

"Rikes!" Scooby shrieked.

"Like, run for it, Scoob!" Shaggy shouted.

Their legs pumped so fast that they were a blur as they raced away from the monster. Outside, the monster followed them from window to window. They ducked down a winding stone stairway and bounded out a door at the bottom.

Breathlessly checking in all directions, they didn't see the monster anywhere. "We did it, Scoob!" Shaggy cried cheerfully. "We're safe and sound!"

He turned and tried to open the door so they could return to the castle, but it wouldn't budge. He pulled hard on the doorknob — no luck. "Like, zoinks!" Shaggy exclaimed unhappily. "I think we just locked ourselves outside the castle."

"Ruh-roh!" Scooby said with a shiver.

"Well, look at the bright side, Scoob," Shaggy told him, trying to be cheerful. "At least it's not raining."

Another deafening boom of thunder sounded and a torrent of soaking rain poured from the sky. Shaggy let out a quick laugh as a drop rolled down his nose. "It'll take more than a rain storm to dampen our spirits."

"ROOAARRRRRR!"

A giant monster, bigger than the castle, blasted its fiery breath at them. It looked like a long-necked red dinosaur with knives for teeth. The monster's eyes glowed yellow through the rain.

"Yikes!" Shaggy screamed.

The monster roared again, sending Shaggy and Scooby racing away. The monster was right behind them, filling the air with its fierce growls and thunderous roars.

Scooby and Shaggy ran around the castle until they found an open door. It led them up a spiral staircase, which they took all the way to the top floor of a round castle tower. But, just when they thought they'd escaped — the monster roared so loud that he blew the top right off the tower!

Shaggy and Scooby screamed as the monster took a giant bite out of the tower. And they yelled even louder when the tower began to topple. They slid down the outside of the tower and crashed right into one of the tents that had been set up for the Highland Games.

"It's still coming after us!" Shaggy yelled.

CHAPTER FIVE

"Guys, what happened?" Fred asked, pulling away the tent material covering Shaggy and Scooby. It was dawn and, from his bedroom window, he'd noticed something moving under a toppled tent out on the field. He'd alerted the rest of the gang and they'd hurried out to see what was going on.

When the tent was off them, Shaggy and Scooby sat up and tried to quit shivering. They weren't able to stop, though. It was cold and, besides, they were scared, wet, and hungry.

With chattering teeth, Shaggy attempted to tell the gang what had happened but he couldn't even get out an entire sentence. "Scooby! Stomach!

Kitchen! Rainstorm! Chase! MON-STER!"

"Reah! RONSTER!" Scooby said, nodding.

Shannon came up alongside the gang. "And I thought we Scottish talked funny," she said when she heard Scooby and Shaggy's babbling.

But the gang knew Scooby and Shaggy so well that they understood what their pals were trying to say. "They went searching for a late-night snack and were chased down here by the monster," Daphne explained to Shannon.

"Thank goodness it went away without hurting them," Fred added.

"*Something* sure made these foot-prints!" Velma pointed to a gigantic, flat hole about five feet deep that had been pounded into the grassy field. It was shaped like an animal's print, with five sharp claw marks dug deeply into the ripped-up grass. And there was a whole trail of prints.

Professor Pembroke hurried out of the castle, eager to learn what was going on. When she saw the enormous footprints, her face lit with a smile.

"This is extraordinary!" she cried excitedly. "Just what I needed." She took a small camera from her jacket pocket and began snapping photos of the prints. "Fantastic," she said as she snapped shots from every angle. "No one could ever dispute this evidence."

Sir Ian came out of the castle next. "Curse me kilts," he huffed, seeming very unhappy about being awakened so early. "Can't a man get a decent night's sleep without —"

He stopped short when he saw what the morning sun was slowly revealing as it rose and spread light across the field. Every tent on the field was toppled. All the goals, posts, and bleachers had been knocked down. Even the grass itself was torn apart.

"Oh, dear me," he cried. "Not the games field!" He suddenly turned and stared at Scooby and Shaggy who were untangling themselves from the fallen tent. "It's ruined!" he shouted at them. "This is an outrage! Look what you've done!"

"Like, it wasn't our fault," Scooby explained. "It tried to eat us! We barely survived!"

"Tell me," requested Sir Ian, interested. "What tried to eat you?"

Shaggy swallowed hard before answering. He didn't even like to think about it. "Like, the Loch Ness Monster."

Sir Ian's face reddened with fury. "For the last time!" he bellowed. "There's no such thing as the Loch Ness Monster!"

"But, Ian, look," Professor Pembroke urged him as she pointed at one of the footprints. "The proof is all around us. And now I have these, the clearest pictures ever taken of the foot —"

"Eeee-nough!" Sir Ian commanded at the top of his voice. He turned to face Shannon. "Miss Blake, I do not wish to spend one more moment at Blake Castle! I'm going to call a cab!" He stormed off in search of a taxi to take him away from Blake Castle.

"Well, that didn't go well," Fred remarked as they watched Sir Ian stomping away angrily.

"I believe you could say that," Shannon agreed.

"Jinkies!" Velma cried softly. Fred, Daphne, and Shannon looked over to where she stood, next to one of the giant footprints. "The footprints," she said. "They don't lead to Loch Ness. They lead into town!"

"Why would a sea monster walk along the road?" Daphne wondered out loud.

"Well, gang," Fred said. "It looks like we have a real mystery on our hands."

Velma nodded. "Only nobody's solved this one in 1,500 years," she added.

A few hours later, the gang and Shannon got out of the Mystery Machine, which Colin and Angus had helped them pull out of the loch. They had decided to follow the monster's footprints and it had led them to a charming town just outside Loch Ness.

"Here we are, gang!" Fred said as they all climbed out of the van. "Welcome to Drumna . . . drumny . . . dramunno . . ." Even though he was trying hard, Fred just couldn't pronounce the strange Scottish name.

"Rrr-Drumnadrochit," Scooby said, saying the name correctly.

"Gesundheit!" Shaggy said, thinking that Scooby had sneezed.

The kids looked around at the old-fashioned stone buildings with their colorful shuttered windows and the cobblestone roads. "This little town is so darned cute!" Daphne commented.

"Like, total grooviness!" Shaggy agreed.

"Reah," Scooby agreed.

At that moment, Angus and Colin Haggart came down the street along with their father, Lachlan Haggart. Colin and Angus struggled to hold onto a giant Loch Ness Monster balloon. Each of them clung to one of its ropes.

"Mr. Haggart, can we have a word with you?" Shannon called.

Lachlan Haggart nodded and came closer to join them. "Now, Miss Blake, what brings ye to town, then?" he asked. "Shouldn't ye be out at the games field keepin' an eye out for more of your scary monster sightings?" he asked with laughter in his voice.

"Laugh if you want," she said to him, "but there may not be any games at all." She took out pictures she'd taken of the wrecked fields. "These pictures were taken early this morning and the games are tomorrow!"

"Ach!" Lachlan Haggart cried. "This is horrible! Disastrous! Catastrophe!"

"Whether you believe in the monster or not, Mr. Haggart, we're running out of time!" Shannon pointed out.

"Right you are, lass!" Mr. Haggart agreed. He beckoned to his sons. "Boys, come quick!"

Colin and Angus handed the balloon ropes to Scooby and Shaggy. "Here you go," said Colin.

"Like, thanks," Shaggy said, taking the rope from him.

"We've got trouble brewing at Blake Castle," Lachlan Haggart told his sons, showing them Shannon's pictures.

As Colin and Angus looked at the

photos, a gust of wind blew through the town, sending the Loch Ness Monster balloon sailing. Shaggy and Scooby held tight to the ropes as they were lifted off their feet by the huge, blowing balloon. "WHOOAAA!!" they screamed.

At that moment, Del Chilton came out of a shop near where the gang and Shannon stood with Mr. Haggart. He strolled over and took a look at the pictures that Shannon was showing Colin and Angus.

"Round up some help and get down to Blake Castle as quick as ye can!" Lachlan Haggart instructed his sons. "The games must go on!" Colin and Angus nodded and ran off down the street.

"Whoa! Stupendous!" Del cried. "Tremendous! Nessie's trying to tell us something! I've got to get to the castle. My monster needs me!" He began to run toward Blake Castle.

"No, Del! Wait!" Shannon shouted as she ran after him.

Del stopped running and faced her. "Waiting time is overs-ville," he said. "She's trying to talk to me and I'm ready to listen!"

"Please, Del," Shannon pleaded. "We don't want word of this to spread! We've still got the games to think about."

"The games?" Del cried. "That's the problem. If it weren't for those games, Nessie would be happy and healthy and mindin' her own business." He started moving in the direction of the castle once again. "I've got to get over to Blake Castle before those Haggart hooligans get there and ruin the vibe, man!" He waved at them. "You guys keep on keepin' on!"

"Well, happy monster-hunting," Fred called to him, returning the wave.

Scooby and Shaggy tied the balloon to two trees and joined the others in the Mystery Machine. At the dock, they found Professor Pembroke's old, broken-down boat. Fred shook his head doubtfully as they climbed onboard. "It doesn't look real seaworthy," he remarked.

"I wish I'd brought my floaties," Shaggy commented as they explored the boat.

"So do I," Velma agreed. "There are only four life jackets on the boat."

Fred bent and tugged on a trapdoor handle in the boat's deck floor. "Maybe there's more down here," he suggested hopefully. He strained and struggled, but the door didn't budge. "It's locked from the inside," he reported, standing.

"That's strange," Velma commented. "I guess two of us will have to stay behind."

In an instant Shaggy and Scooby were beside Fred and Velma, saluting eagerly. "Shaggy and Scooby volunteering for shore duty!" Shaggy announced.

"Raye-raye, raptain!" Scooby agreed.

"You mean split up and search for clues?" Fred asked. "I like it!"

"Hey! Maybe Shaggy and Scooby should take the Mystery Machine," Daphne suggested.

"Good idea!" Fred said enthusiastically. Then he realized what he had just said. "What?" Fred was the only one Fred trusted enough to drive the Mystery Machine.

"Don't worry, Fred. We won't get a scratch on her," Shaggy assured him as they hurried off the boat. Shaggy and Scooby jumped into the Mystery Machine.

Velma just shook her head as the van jerked forward, then sped away. "Suddenly, this boat seems like a much safer place," she said.

CHAPTER SIX

Fred quickly stopped worrying about Shaggy driving the Mystery Machine. He was too excited about driving the big boat out onto the lake. "I'm taking her to full throttle!" he said, standing in front of the boat's steering wheel. "Let's see what this baby can do!"

Fred pulled the boat away from the dock and headed out onto Loch Ness. He pushed the throttle forward, sending the boat speeding even faster. "Whoo hoo! I'm king of the loch!" he shouted gleefully.

Shannon, Daphne, and Velma went below to the control room. Velma turned dials on the boat's old-fashioned sonar tracking equipment. "Anything coming up on the sonar, Velma?" Daphne asked.

"Are you kidding?" Velma replied. "This sonar system is so old, it couldn't pick up a radio station."

"That's strange," Shannon commented. "I know Professor Pembroke's research funding is limited, but she's obviously not spending *any* of it on new equipment."

Suddenly, a blip appeared on the sonar screen. "Hey! We might have something!" Daphne cried. She leaned in to get a better look at the sonar screen. "There's a large target off the port side bow," she reported.

All at once, the screen went blank! "Oh no!" Shannon shouted. "We've lost the signal."

Velma, Daphne, and Shannon ran to the upper deck to see if they could locate whatever it was that had shown up on the sonar screen. They could see something large moving along the water's surface at the front left side of the boat. "It's her!" Shannon shouted. "She's back!"

Velma and Daphne didn't have to ask who *she* was. Just then, the boat was bumped hard by something underneath it.

"Freddy, now would be a good time for one of your famous plans!" Daphne cried.

Fred thought hard. "Uuuuhh." Then his eyes brightened and he snapped his fingers as a plan occurred to him. "Got it!" he announced. "Throw all the nets overboard!"

Daphne stared at Fred with a doubtful expression on her face. "You mean this little boat is going to catch that gigantic monster?" she asked.

"That's plan A," Fred told her, nodding.

Daphne, Shannon, and Velma tossed the nets over the side. In only a few minutes, the boat lurched forward. "It looks like we got a bite!" Velma shouted.

It was unbelievable! They'd actually netted the Loch Ness Monster! "Ooookay!" Fred cheered.

But their triumphant smiles faded as the powerful creature dragged the boat forward at an incredible speed, knocking them off their feet. "Whoooahhh!" they all shouted, clutching onto the sides of the boat.

Something clanged and slid across the boat's deck, smashing into the back railing. "We just lost the engine," Velma shouted.

The boat leaned hard to the right. "She went under the boat and disappeared," Shannon shouted, hanging over the side to see. The monster was out of sight, but it was still attached to the boat — and she was dragging them down to the bottom of the lake!

Shaggy looked out the window as he drove the Mystery Machine along a steep, rutted road. He was beginning to suspect that he and Scooby were lost. He must have made a wrong turn on his way up the mountain to Blake Castle. "Like, are things getting creepier and spookier, or is it just me?" he asked Scooby.

"Rit's re, roo," Scooby replied, nodding.

Shaggy looked up at the sky, which was growing darker every second. "Like, Scoob, ol' buddy, I've got a feeling we're not in Coolsville anymore," he remarked.

Suddenly, the front wheel of the Mystery Machine banged into something. "Huh?" Shaggy cried.

He gripped the steering wheel as the front end of the van dipped down into a rut. The engine whirred while the wheels spun in place. "Zoinks, like, I think we're stuck!" he said.

He pushed open the door and climbed out. He and Scooby walked to the front of the van. "Wow! Look at the size of that pothole!" Shaggy remarked as he examined the hole the Mystery Machine had crashed into.

When Shaggy looked for Scooby, he was gone. "Hey!" he cried, checking for him in every direction. Finally, he spotted Scooby running down the road. "Scoob!" he called to him. "Come back here, you dingy dog!"

Scooby checked back over his shoulder, but he didn't stop running. Instead, he whimpered and pointed at something behind Shaggy.

"ROOAARRRRR!!!!"

Shaggy's shoulders tensed up to his ears. He didn't have to turn to know what was behind him. And he suddenly realized what the van had driven into — it was a gigantic footprint made by the Loch Ness Monster!

In the next second, Shaggy raced into the Mystery Machine, turned the key, and pressed all the way down on the gas pedal. The wheels spun and the van lurched forward, out of the pit.

"ROOAARRRR!!!!"

The monster swooped down over the van, its giant jaws snapping.

Shaggy sped up the road alongside Scooby. Reaching out the window, he yanked Scooby by the collar and pulled him into the van. Scooby curled up in the passenger's seat, too terrified to look out the window.

The monster jumped in front of the Mystery Machine. Shaggy jammed on the brakes. The wheels squealed, but the van kept sliding forward. In another moment, they'd drive right into the creature's open, waiting jaws!

Shaggy threw himself on the steering wheel, pulling hard to the right. The Mystery Machine went up on two wheels, but it managed to turn just as the Loch Ness Monster chomped down.

Once again, Shaggy hit the gas pedal hard. He didn't let off the gas for a second. He knew he needed to put as much space as he could between the van and the monster. The Mystery Machine bounced over rocks. It smashed fallen branches and shot gravel from under its wheels as it raced away from the monster.

After a few minutes, Shaggy looked in the rearview mirror. He didn't see the monster. "Like, I think we lost her," he told Scooby.

But something wasn't right.

The bumpy road didn't seem bumpy anymore. In fact, he couldn't feel the road at all. "What happened to the road?" he asked in a panicky voice.

Shaggy and Scooby both looked out the window, searching for the road beneath them. They quickly saw what had happened to it. The road had disappeared!

They'd driven off a cliff!

"Like, Houston, we have a problem!" Shaggy shouted as the van plummeted into the lake below. "Mayday! Mayday! Mayday!"

Fred looked up from the deck of the boat. "That sounds like Shaggy!" he said. He checked in every direction. "Shaggy? Where are you?" he called.

"Like, incoming!" he heard Shaggy shout.

He checked his walkie-talkie. Was Shaggy trying to contact him?

The next thing Fred and the others knew, the Mystery Machine was coming in for a crash landing — right on the deck of Professor Pembroke's boat!

SMASH! BANG! CRASH!

"Somebody get that guy's license,"

Fred muttered dizzily as he got up from under a pile of broken wood.

"Reah, roggy ricense," Scooby said. He and Shaggy staggered out of the van.

"At least everyone's all right," Daphne said.

"And the crash broke the ropes that were keeping us tied to the monster," Velma added.

"Monster?" Shaggy asked. "How could the monster have been down here when we just saw it up there?"

"I don't know," Velma admitted. "But I think we'd better go find out."

Although Professor Pembroke's old boat was now very battered, the kids managed to get it to the dock. Then they drove back up the mountain to where Shaggy and Scooby had met up with the Loch Ness Monster. "These

monster tracks turn into tire tracks,"
Velma noticed as she followed the
giant prints along the road.

"Hmm," Velma said thoughtfully. "It
looks like the monster isn't the only
mystery around here."

CHAPTER SEVEN

Back at the dock, the gang and Shannon told Professor Pembroke about what had happened to her boat and apologized for the damage.

"Well, don't worry yourselves none," Professor Pembroke told them. "It was all in the name of research and it sounds like you had quite the sighting."

"Sighting!" Shaggy cried. "My eyes were closed the whole time."

"Re, roo!" Shaggy admitted.

"At least the game field is looking good as new," Shannon said.

"I guess we owe the Haggart brothers a hearty thanks," Fred said.

"Yeah, but where are they?" Velma wondered.

Daphne used the ship's magnetic arm to knock over the monster that had trapped Shaggy and Scooby. Inside, they found Angus and Colin, playing another one of their practical jokes!

When they looked inside the metallic lake monster, the kids found Professor Pembroke at the controls! She'd wanted to convince Sir Ian that the monster existed, so she played a trick on all of them.

Now that the mystery had been solved, the Highland Games could begin on the bonnie banks of Loch Ness! "Rooby-rooby-roo!" cheered Scooby.

"Those jokers?" Shannon said with a rueful sigh. "If goofing off were a Highland Games event, Colin and Angus would be champions, for sure."

"Speaking of goofing off," Shaggy said. "Where's Scooby?" He saw Scooby at the end of the dock and walked down to join him. Scooby was looking out at the lake with a long spyglass he'd found on Professor Pembroke's boat. "Like, way to go, Scoob!" Shaggy praised him. "That demon from the depths can't sneak up on us if we keep an eye out for her."

"Ruh-huh," Scooby agreed.

Shaggy took the spyglass from Scooby. "Let me have a peek," he said. He looked through the spyglass, but he was holding it backwards. Instead of making everything look closer, like it was supposed to do, the backward spyglass made everything appear farther away than it was. "Hey, look at that!" he cried. "There's a groovy ship way out there on the loch," he told Scooby.

But Scooby saw that the ship was much, much closer than Shaggy thought. In fact, it was about to crash right into them! "Raggy! Rook!" he shouted.

"Zoinks!" Shaggy yelled as a large ship crashed right into the dock, splintering it.

"Ahoy there!" Sir Ian called to them from the open upper deck of his luxurious ship. He looked over the side and saw that he'd crashed into the dock. "Oh, dear, dear!" he fretted. "I'm terribly sorry about that Miss Blake."

"That's quite all right, Sir Ian,"

Shannon called up to him from what remained of the dock.

"Well, well, well, Sir Ian Locksley," Professor Pembroke called up to him. "What are you doing out here on the loch? Does this mean you're a Nessie true believer, after all?"

"Believer? Nonsense!" he scoffed. "I'm here to protect the games field! I'm going to patrol the waters to make sure nothing else . . . *peculiar* . . . happens. Loch Ness is now under my command!"

"You can't do that!" Professor Pembroke said.

"I can! And I will!" Sir Ian declared firmly. "I hereby command that no boat other than mine is to be allowed near Blake Castle!"

Professor Pembroke snorted disdainfully. "And how could you stop me?" she asked.

"By having that floating scrap pile condemned!" he replied. "Now I suggest that you finish your repairs and be on your way! Your friends can take a ride on my boat if they like. I'm sure they'll find it much more comfortable."

"Oh, blow it out your bagpipe!" Professor Pembroke yelled up at him. "This boat has more surprises in her than you'll ever know," she shouted as she walked toward her boat.

Velma took hold of her arm. "Err . . . Professor Pembroke," she said. "Perhaps we *should* go with Sir Ian to search for more clues."

"Brilliant!" the professor agreed. "It may be that we'll make a true believer out of him yet!"

Sir Ian was glad to welcome Shannon and the gang onto his boat. Once his ship left the dock, he showed them around. They were impressed with all the gadgets and gizmos he had in his grand control room. "This sure is impressive equipment," Velma complimented him.

Velma sat by the ship's sonar panel and opened her personal laptop computer. She began typing on the keyboard. After a moment, she stopped to explain what she was doing. "I've networked my laptop into the ship's computer. This way I can monitor the sonar and download information."

"Suit yourselves," Sir Ian said with a shrug of his bony shoulders. He switched on his sonar tracking device. It looked like a large table, but there was a screen where the tabletop would have been.

Velma's laptop, which was now hooked up to the ship's computer, began beeping. "Say hello to the Ocean Motion 3000," Sir Ian said proudly. "With it, we can track our position by satellite while scanning the bottom of Loch Ness at the same time."

At that moment, something bumped the boat. Sir Ian turned to a tall crew member, his second-in-command. "McIntyre, report!" he commanded.

"We've been hit by something that's nearly 20 meters long," the man told him.

"I see it on your sonar," Daphne pointed out.

"I saw it, too," said Shannon. "And now it's suddenly disappeared off the screen."

Sir Ian studied the sonar screen. "Something that size cannot just vanish! There must be some explanation!"

"Whatever it was, it's probably hiding in an underwater cave," Velma said.

"Aye," Shannon agreed. "Loch Ness is famous for them."

"I wish there was some way we could check it out," Fred said.

They returned to the open upper deck and got there just in time to see Scooby and Shaggy sneaking into a large, round, metal craft. "I must say, it looks like your friends fancy my mini submarine," Sir Ian observed.

"Those chickens must be trying to hide from the monster in there," Velma suggested.

"That mini sub would be perfect for

exploring the loch," Shannon said. "Do you think we could borrow it, Sir Ian?"

"I don't know," Sir Ian replied. "Do you think you could pilot such a craft?"

"I could," Fred assured him. "I drove my van into the loch just yesterday."

The gang and Shannon quickly joined Scooby and Shaggy inside the compact submarine.

"Next time, I pick the hiding place," Shaggy told Scooby.

There was just barely room for all of them. A magnetic arm controlled by Sir Ian's crewmember, McIntyre, stretched out over the lake. The large metal, magnetic gripper on the edge of the steel arm opened and dropped them down into the lake below.

"Wahoo! Cool!" Fred cheered as they hit the water and kept sinking down into the depths of Loch Ness. "This thing is great. All it needs is a styling green paint job and it'll be da bomb-diggity!"

"It even has a sonar activated camera," Velma said, testing the sub's various controls. "If anything passes in front of the sub, an image will immediately be transmitted to the ship above."

Fred piloted the ship through the lake without any problem. "Now all we need is to find the entrance to the underwater caves," he said.

Daphne and Shannon peered out the window at the front of the sub. "It's darker down here than I thought it would be," Daphne commented.

"Aye, Loch Ness is also known for its murky depths," Shannon explained, "which makes it near impossible to navigate through."

Just then a group of eels appeared in the window and startled Scooby. "Ronsters!" he shouted. He jumped up onto Fred's back, wrapping his big paws over Fred's eyes.

"Look out, Scooby," Fred cried as he steered blindly, crashing through a cluster of rock. The sub hit an underwater boulder and bounced off.

"Fred, watch where you're going!" Daphne cried.

"I would if I could," Fred replied, trying to pry Scooby's paws off his eyes. The sub hit the bottom of the lake and then bounced up before settling on a rock ledge.

Daphne suddenly leaned forward and looked out the window. "Look, guys," she said. "I think we found the entrance."

"And I thought it would be impossible," Shannon commented.

"Well, nothing's impossible when you've got Scooby-Doo around," Daphne said, smiling at Scooby.

"Raw, rucks," Scooby said, blushing modestly.

Fred took the sub through twisting, turning passages in the cave. After a few minutes, he had the feeling that they were in shallow water, but they weren't near the lake's surface. He turned on the sub's front floodlight. He took the sub up until they were above the surface of the water.

When they realized what they were looking at, Shannon and the gang gasped. They'd come up into an immense stone cavern. Although the entire cavern was underwater, there was air and dry land inside of it.

They climbed out of the sub and stepped onto the dry land. Scooby caught a scent and sniffed, following the trail until he found a very big bone. Shaggy came alongside him and when he saw the bone he called to the others. "Hey, gang, you might want to check this out."

When Fred, Velma, Daphne, and Shannon arrived with their flashlights, they saw a ghastly sight. All around them sat skeletons dressed in ancient armor, complete with swords, shields, and helmets. "I think we've stumbled across a burial ground used by ancient Scottish warriors," Velma said. The gang and Shannon flashed their lights all over, studying the spooky burial site.

Shaggy and Scooby disappeared behind a boulder for a moment. When
they returned, they were dressed in
helmets and shields and waved ancient swords. "Hey, guys, look at us!"
Shaggy called to Shannon and the
rest of the gang. "We're a couple of
brave warriors."

"Reah, rave rarriors," Scooby said,
holding up his sword proudly.

Velma picked something metallic up
from the ground. "Take a look at this,"
she said. "It's a screwdriver." She held
it up for all of them to see. "But what's
it doing down here?"

"Maybe they were handy ancient people?" Fred guessed.

"Freddy!" Velma scolded. "What
would ancient warriors be doing with
a modern screwdriver?"

"Um . . . guys," Shaggy said in a

quivering voice. "If you think that's fishy — just look behind you!"

They all turned at once and gasped. The Loch Ness Monster had stuck its huge, monstrous head into the cave.

"Get to the submarine!" Fred shouted.

They ran to the sub, but the monster cut off Shaggy and Scooby's path to the sub with its long neck. "Ro-no!" Scooby shouted.

"We're trapped, Scoob!" Shaggy cried. "We'll have to make like these brave Scottish warriors and fight." He thrust his sword at the monster. "Like get ready to fight McShaggy and Scooby-McDoo!" he cried.

The monster lunged at them — and Shaggy threw his sword in the air and ran! "Like, let's get out of here," Shaggy yelled to Scooby. Scooby tossed his sword away and followed him.

"This place is a real *dive!*" Shaggy shouted as they jumped in the water and swam to the sub.

The moment Scooby and Shaggy reached the sub and scrambled inside, Fred brought it underwater and sped out of the cave the same way they'd come in. From there, he was able to steer the sub back into the open lake water.

But the Loch Ness Monster stayed right behind them. "It's following us!" Velma reported in a worried voice.

"Well, at least we can get a good picture of old Nessie," Fred said.

"No, we can't," Velma disagreed. "The sonar camera is mounted on the front of the sub. We'll have to turn around if we're going to do a photo shoot."

Shaggy checked out the window. "That thing is gaining on us," he informed them. "I wouldn't recommend it!"

They came to a stone canyon wall, and Fred headed straight up the side of it. "We've just lost our sonar camera," Daphne informed him as she watched the control panel. "The camera must have been knocked off the ship when we hit the canyon wall."

Velma kept her eye on the sonar screen. The monster was still behind them. "Twenty-five more meters," she said. "It's a straight shot to the surface!"

"Fred, look out!" Daphne suddenly screamed.

"I see it!" he yelled in reply. The monster had come around the side of the sub and gotten in front of them.

Nessie was heading straight at the mini sub with her jaws wide open.

Velma still had her eye on the sonar screen. "She's going to ram us!" she shouted.

"Hang on!" Fred told them. He steered the sub out of the monster's path just as it was about to smash into them. Fred turned all the sub's switches on full power, sending the sub zooming to the surface.

"Whoooooaaaa!" they all yelled at once.

Scooby and Shaggy felt suddenly sick from the sudden motion — and even sicker when the mini sub shot straight up out of the water and into the air. "Like, who knew we could get airsick in a submarine," Shaggy said.

"Rurp," Scooby belched.

The magnetic arm of Sir Ian's boat

extended out to grab hold of them. Its magnet attracted the ship to it and the arm's grippers clamped shut around it. They were pulled to safety back aboard the boat.

"Like, can we go home now?" Shaggy asked.

CHAPTER EIGHT

By the time Shannon and the gang returned to the dock, the sun was setting. "Well, gang," Fred said as they headed back to the Mystery Machine, "with the games starting tomorrow, we'd better get some sleep."

"Yeah, like I'd hate to be tired and cranky during the monster's final rampage," Shaggy quipped wearily.

"We can't go to bed yet," Velma protested. "There are too many unanswered questions."

"I've got one," Daphne said. "What is that sound?" They all listened and heard a low rumble coming from the back of the van. Fred yanked the doors open and they saw Del Chilton sleeping in the back.

He awoke with a start, rubbing his eyes. "Oh, sorry, guys," he said. "I was at the castle, you know, trying to connect with Nessie's energy, and somebody ripped off my van."

"Your van's been stolen?" Velma cried.

"From Blake Castle?" Shannon asked, unable to believe her ears.

"Like, wow, it seemed like such a good neighborhood," Shaggy remarked.

"Listen, gang," Velma said as all of them climbed into the Mystery Machine and Fred started it up. "We've got to solve this mystery tonight and I know just the person to help us do it!" She took the van's handheld radio and tried to contact Professor Pembroke on her boat. "She's not answering," she told the others. "Maybe she went out onto the deck and she's out of range."

"She shouldn't be on the loch alone," Shannon remarked, "especially to-night."

"Maybe she's tracking the monster there," Fred suggested.

"Like . . . I don't think so!" Shaggy shouted. A moment later, they all saw exactly what he meant! The Loch Ness Monster was staring right into the van at them.

"ROAARRR!"

The kids screamed as Fred gunned the motor and shot past the monster. The van screeched around the sharp corners of the mountain road.

"We've got another turn, hold on!" Fred warned them. But he was go-ing too fast to keep the van on the road, and it careened into a nearby field.

The Mystery Machine bounced along at top speed, completely out of control. It knocked down an old well and smashed into an abandoned old stone house — and out the other side.

The Loch Ness Monster roared furiously behind them. No matter how fast Fred drove, he couldn't shake the monster.

"Fred, you're heading right for a peat bog!" Daphne warned.

"You mean an area of partially decayed, partly rotted roots, branches, leaves and seeds?" Velma asked.

"Exactly!" Daphne cried as the van headed straight for the muddy patch of land.

"She's coming!" Shannon shouted, checking the rearview mirror. The monster was closing in. In minutes it would be right on top of them.

Fred slammed on the brakes, but it was too late. The Mystery Machine sped into the peat bog and stuck fast in the gooey, organic sludge. The monster raced into the bog after them and stuck fast!

Del sprang out of the van. "This is the moment I've been waiting for my whole life!" he shouted joyfully. But he was soon bewildered as the monster lurched forward and leaned heavily to one side. It wasn't behaving like a living creature at all.

Fred got out of the van behind him. "I think we need to take a closer look at this monster," he said.

The gang, Shannon, and Del slogged through the thick, squishy bog and made their way over to the monster.

Daphne touched it and pulled her hand back, surprised by how dry its skin felt. "Jeepers!" she cried. "This is one sea serpent that could sure use some moisturizer."

Fred touched it, too. "That's not skin, it's canvas," he said. They all reached for the monster and realized Fred was right. It was made of canvas tarp. Together, they pulled the material down. Underneath, they found Del's stolen van.

Daphne opened the door to the van. "There's no one inside," she said with a gasp.

"They must have escaped," Shannon suggested.

Fred knelt and inspected the tire marks coming from Del's van. "Check it out, gang," he said. "Del's treads match the tire tracks we found earlier."

"So someone's been using my wheels to fake us out this whole time?" Del asked.

"But this doesn't add up," Daphne pointed out. "Del's van couldn't have chased us through the underwater tunnels."

"Or attacked us on the boat," Fred added.

"And Shaggy and Scooby were chased by the creature last night," Shannon reminded them, "before Del's van was stolen. This can only mean one thing."

"More than one monster," Fred said.

Del smiled brightly. "So Nessie's still out there!"

"Nessie or no Nessie, this van hoax proves that somebody's behind at least part of this mystery," Velma said. "There's only one thing left to do . . ."

"Like, take a two-week vacation to a tropical paradise?" Shaggy suggested hopefully. Scooby nodded eagerly.

"No, you chickens," Velma told them. "We've got to head back to Blake Castle. I've got a plan."

CHAPTER NINE

It was foggy that night. Velma could barely see the moon as she stood on a high wall of Blake Castle and contacted Fred on her walkie-talkie. "Fred, how's the trap coming?"

Fred was down at the cove, along the lake shore. "Roger that, mama bird," he replied, speaking into his walkie-talkie. "This is baby bird. We copy. We are go. Repeat. We are go. Alpha. Bravo. Charlie. Baby bird. Over."

Del, who was on the dock beside Fred, took the walkie-talkie and told Velma what she really wanted to know. "We're ready, Velma," he said. "But the fog is rolling in fast."

"Uh-oh," Velma said. "I can't see

Shaggy and Scooby anymore." Looking through binoculars, she peered down to the lake where Scooby and Shaggy rowed in a small row boat. They were there as decoys, to lure the Loch Ness Monster out of hiding. Velma tried to reach them on the walkie-talkies. "Velma to Shaggy. Come in. Are you two okay?"

"Negatory on that!" Shaggy responded over his walkie-talkie. He and Scooby were dressed as fishermen in yellow hats and slickers. "Like, we're all out of Scooby Snacks!" Scooby whimpered to let Velma know how bad the problem was.

On Sir Ian's ship, Daphne and Shannon kept a close watch on the sonar screen. Something big suddenly appeared on the screen. "There it is again," Shannon noticed. "It's heading right into the cove."

Sir Ian came to look at the screen. "Good gravy!" he cried when he saw the immense size of the moving object they were tracking.

"I'll call Velma," Daphne volunteered, taking out her walkie-talkie.

McIntyre, Sir Ian's second-in-command, stepped forward and snatched Daphne's walkie-talkie from her. "Oh, no. Let's not be hasty," he said roughly.

"McIntyre, what's going on?" Sir Ian demanded.

"Forgive me, Sir Ian," McIntyre said. "But I've come up with a little plan of my own. I intend to capture that creature and sell it for quite a handsome amount of cash. I'll split the money with my helpers."

The three other crew members stepped forward and held Sir Ian, Shannon, and Daphne tightly. "How are you going to catch it?" Daphne demanded.

McIntyre gestured toward a sharp, barbed harpoon attached to a large spool of heavy rope. "The old-fashioned way," he answered.

Out on the lake, in the cove near the castle, Scooby and Shaggy sat in their rowboat, waiting for the Loch Ness Monster to appear.

"Like, I'd like to see old fang fins sneak up on us, right old buddy?" said Shaggy.

Scooby laughed. "Rang rins," he said, enjoying the joke.

Meanwhile, Velma had spotted the monster swimming into the cove. She radioed to Fred, alerting him that it was approaching. "The monster is in the cove," she radioed. "Repeat. The monster is in the cove."

Del and Fred sprang into action. "Tie off your end, Del," Fred instructed. "I'm going across."

Del had parked his van a few yards away. He quickly tied one end of a long, strong rope net to its back bumper.

At the same time, Fred jumped into a small boat with an outboard motor. He grabbed the other end of the rope net and sped across the cove to the dock on the other side of the cove. Once he got there, he tied the net to the dock's mooring post. Now they had the Loch Ness Monster trapped in the cove.

From her position on the castle wall, Velma saw the monster dive under the water and swim up directly underneath Scooby and Shaggy's little rowboat. It came up and lifted them high into the air. In the darkness and thick fog, they didn't realize they were sitting on the monster's head!

Velma radioed to warn them. "Shaggy, come in," she spoke into the walkie-talkie. "It's beneath you!"

"Yes, I've always thought being live bait was beneath us, too," Shaggy replied, not understanding Velma's meaning. "But it's nice to hear someone else say it for a change."

"Listen to me!" she insisted. "Your boat is on top of the monster's head!"

Slowly, with a queasy, nervous feeling, Shaggy peered over the side of the boat. Scooby looked, too. They swallowed hard when they saw the monster below them. "Velma, like I think we found the monster," Shaggy squeaked into his walkie-talkie.

Fred saw what was happening and zoomed up in his motorboat. "Hang on, guys, help is on the way!"

Shaggy turned to Scooby. "You heard him, Scoob. Hang on." As he spoke, the rowboat slipped off the monster's head and slid down its long neck. "WHOOAA!!" Scooby and Shaggy shouted together. The boat hit the water with a loud splash. The monster went after it as it floated out into the lake — and swam right into the net Del and Fred had spread.

Fred contacted Velma on the walkie-talkie. "Our trap worked!" he cried happily.

But Velma could see something that

he hadn't noticed yet. "Freddy, look behind you," she warned. Sir Ian's ship was now cruising right into the cove at top speed. It was heading straight for the net, the dock — and for Fred!

CHAPTER TEN

On the upper deck of Sir Ian's ship, McIntyre's thuggish helper aimed his harpoon at the monster trapped in the net. "Target in range," he told McIntyre.

"Excellent. Stand by for my command," McIntyre commanded him.

Daphne saw that McIntyre and his three thugs were all paying attention to what was going on in the lake — and not to her and Shannon. Daphne caught Shannon's eye and her cousin seemed to understand what Daphne had in mind. Together, they elbowed their captors hard in the stomach. With grunts of pain, the thugs let go of Daphne and Shannon.

"Fire!" McIntyre gave the command.

The harpoonist got ready to fire.

The two cousins ran to the edge of the upper deck. Below, they could see Fred in his small motorboat. "Watch out, Freddy!" Daphne shouted. "He's got a harpoon!"

But Fred didn't seem to hear her, and there wasn't time for him to get out of the ship's path.

Thinking fast, Daphne snapped up her purse off a nearby table. She threw it over a rope leading to the harpoonist, clutching the handles with one hand and the bag with the other. With Shannon hanging on, they slid down the rope to the harpoonist as he was about to fire.

THUD!

They crashed into him, pushing him aside and sending the harpoon gun spinning. The shot he fired went wild, completely missing the Loch Ness Monster and shooting the harpoon all the way up to Blake Castle. Velma ducked as the harpoon cracked the castle wall right behind her head.

In the excitement, McIntyre forgot about steering the ship. It smashed into the dock, blasting a path even further into the rocky shore behind the dock.

"Whooooaaa!" Fred shouted as his small boat was tossed out of the water by the waves created by the ship's crash. The impact of the collision also threw McIntyre and his men off the boat, along with Sir Ian. All of them fell, shouting and splashing, into the lake below. Only Shannon and Daphne managed to hang on.

The waves sent Scooby and Shaggy's rowboat speeding to the shore. Shaggy barely got out of the boat fast enough. He jumped out into the water and — using the oars as stilts — ran the rest of the way to dry land with Scooby on his back.

"Help!" Sir Ian shouted as he splashed about frantically in the lake. "Throw me a line! I can't swim!"

Up on the ship, Daphne and Shannon heard his voice. "We've got to do something!" Shannon said.

Daphne had an idea. She remembered the magnetic arm that had gripped the mini submarine. Hurrying to the controls she began to activate the arm, hoping to pluck him up out of the lake.

As Daphne lowered the arm, Sir Ian struggled in the water. Suddenly, he sensed something coming through the fog at him. Looking up, he saw the giant face of the Loch Ness Monster staring down at him through the fog. For a moment, he was so stunned, he forgot that he was drowning. "My word!" he shouted. "I don't believe my eyes! She *is* real!"

As the arm extended, the Loch Ness Monster began to rise up. It was being pulled by the giant magnet. In seconds the monster was caught in the arm's metallic grip.

"Whoever heard of a magnet stopping a sea monster?" Shannon asked.

Fred zoomed in on his boat and plucked Sir Ian from the water. He looked around and sighed with relief. Everything seemed to be working out okay.

But just when they thought they had the monster in their magnetic clutches, Shaggy and Scooby came running, screaming, down the shore. Another Loch Ness Monster was after them.

Velma was coming down the cliff when she saw that the second Loch Ness Monster was about to chase Scooby and Shaggy right into the pit they'd dug as a trap. "Look out, guys!" she shouted.

"Help!" Shaggy yelled. "Like, this place is infested with monsters!"

"That's where we set the . . ." But it was too late. Shaggy and Scooby ran over the pit and crashed down into it. The monster crashed in, right behind them. ". . . trap," Velma finished. She hurried over to see if they were hurt.

"Scooby? Shaggy? Are you okay?" Velma called, peering into the pit.

Shaggy and Scooby crawled out from under the monster. "Terrific, considering we're squished under the Loch Ness Monster," Shaggy replied.

Velma saw two other people escaping from the monster and suddenly realized who they were. Scooby and Shaggy noticed them, too. "Colin and Angus Haggart!" Shaggy cried out in surprise.

"Roar," Colin said.

"So, if this Loch Ness Monster is a fake, like . . . what about that one hanging in the air?" Shaggy asked.

Up on the ship, Daphne was wondering the same thing. "Time for this monster to hit the beach," she told Shannon as she pointed the magnetic arm over the beach and dropped it.

SMASH!

The monster fell and broke. And inside it was a person controlling a mini sub shaped like a monster. Everyone gasped when they saw who it was!

CHAPTER ELEVEN

"Professor Fiona Pembroke!" the gang cried all at once. Del and Shannon gasped and Sir Ian covered his mouth in surprise.

"It's all very simple," Velma explained, as the whole mystery suddenly became clear to her. "Professor Pembroke has been behind this all along."

"She did a good job," Shaggy said. "Scoob and me have been scared all along!"

"But how on earth did she do it?" Shannon asked.

Velma remembered how Fred had tried to open the hatch on the professor's boat but it had been locked from inside. She started to understand how Professor Pembroke had worked it all out. "The locked hatch we found aboard her vessel was actually a secret passageway."

Fred realized what Velma was thinking. "It led to the homemade monster sub that she kept docked beneath her boat."

Velma nodded. "She'd simply climb down the hatch and pedal off into the lake."

Daphne was the next one to understand what had happened. "That way she was free to do her scaring while we all thought she was on the boat."

"But why did she do it?" Shannon asked.

"It wasn't you she was after, or any of us," Velma answered. "It was really Sir Ian's attention that she wanted."

"Me?" Sir Ian cried in amazement.

"What do I have to do with any of this?"

Professor Pembroke had climbed out of the monster sub and now joined the group on the shore. Everyone stared at her as Fred continued the explanation. "She was using fake monsters to get you to believe in a real one, Sir Ian."

"Exactly," Velma told Sir Ian. "She wanted you to become a Nessie true believer. But she couldn't count on Nessie making an appearance, so she created her own."

"And she hired Angus and Colin to help her," Daphne added.

"I bet they wanted to scare away the other athletes so they could win the games," Velma said.

"Not so!" Angus protested. "We don't even care about the games. We just like a good practical joke."

"That monster thing's the greatest joke we ever pulled," Colin agreed.

Velma rolled her eyes as the brothers doubled over with laughter. "So, these guys had their fun by helping Professor Pembroke — all so she could make Sir Ian believe in her work."

"It's true," Professor Pembroke admitted. "Sir Ian would never have looked at my new photos unless he came to believe in the beast."

"She had to find a way to convince him, and the Highland Games at Blake Castle offered her the perfect opportunity."

Once they had all dried off, they followed Sir Ian back into his ship to help him check the damage. McIntyre and his helpers were gone, but Sir Ian had called the local police and was sure they would soon pick them up.

"All your controls seem to be working," Velma said to Sir Ian as she checked different dials. Suddenly, something large appeared on the sonar screen. "The sonar camera that fell off the mini sub is still transmitting a signal," Velma told them.

"Something must have passed in front of the lens and reactivated the sonar sensor," Fred suggested.

"Can you get a fix on the signal?" Professor Pembroke asked.

Velma began reading the coordinates. "Quadrant four. Depth, one hundred and four fathoms."

Professor Pembroke's eyes went wide. "But . . . that's over six hundred feet below."

"Much too deep for any homemade sub to survive," Shannon put in.

Sir Ian joined them, an interested expression on his face. "It can't possibly be?" he said.

Velma nudged the professor. "Show him your pictures," she whispered.

Professor Pembroke reached into her shoulder bag and produced the photos. She handed them to Sir Ian who studied them carefully. "Great Scott!" he cried.

"Sir Ian, does this mean you believe me?" the professor asked hopefully.

Del looked at the photos excitedly. "These are great!" he cried.

"Grab your bags, both of you," Sir Ian commanded Del and Professor Pembroke. "We've got a lot of work ahead of us! We don't want to lose her again!"

"Aye! Aye, man!" Del saluted eagerly.

"Well, it looks like you've got another mystery on your hands," Fred said to the professor.

"And none of this would have been possible without you meddling kids," she said gratefully.

"We try," Scooby told her.

Sir Ian, Del, and Professor Pembroke headed out in search of the real Loch Ness Monster. Shannon looked at the gang and smiled. "Tomorrow's Highland Games are going to be great . . . thanks to you, cousin Daphne, and your great friends." She gathered them together in a group hug.

Scooby popped his head up out of the hug and grinned. Their adventure at Blake Castle had turned out a-okay. "Rooby-rooby-roo," he cheered.